SHERLOCK CHICK AND THE GIANT EGG MYSTERY

To librarians, parents, and teachers:

Sherlock Chick and the Giant Egg Mystery is a Parents Magazine READ ALOUD Original — one title in a series of colorfully illustrated and fun-to-read stories that young readers will be sure to come back to time and time again.

Now, in this special school and library edition of *Sherlock Chick and the Giant Egg Mystery,* adults have an even greater opportunity to increase children's responsiveness to reading and learning — and to have fun every step of the way.

When you finish this story, check the special section at the back of the book. There you will find games, projects, things to talk about, and other educational activities designed to make reading enjoyable by giving children and adults a chance to play together, work together, and talk over the story they have just read.

For a free color catalog describing Gareth Stevens' list of high-quality books, call 1-800-341-3569 (USA) or 1-800-461-9120 (Canada).

Parents Magazine READ ALOUD Originals:

Golly Gump Swallowed a Fly
The Housekeeper's Dog
Who Put the Pepper in the Pot?
Those Terrible Toy-Breakers
The Ghost in Dobbs Diner
The Biggest Shadow in the Zoo
The Old Man and the Afternoon Cat
Septimus Bean and His Amazing Machine
Sherlock Chick's First Case
A Garden for Miss Mouse
Witches Four
Bread and Honey

Pigs in the House
Milk and Cookies
But No Elephants
No Carrots for Harry!
Snow Lion
Henry's Awful Mistake
The Fox with Cold Feet
Get Well, Clown-Arounds!
Pets I Wouldn't Pick
Sherlock Chick and the Giant
   Egg Mystery

Library of Congress Cataloging-in-Publication Data

Quackenbush, Robert M.
    Sherlock Chick and the giant egg mystery / by Robert Quackenbush. — North American library ed.
        p. cm. — (Parents magazine read aloud original)
    Summary: Sherlock Chick tries to solve the mystery of the giant egg that arrives at the farm.
    ISBN 0-8368-0897-5
    [1. Chickens—Fiction. 2. Eggs—Fiction. 3. Farm life—Fiction. 4. Mystery and detective stories.] I.
Title. II. Series.
    PZ7.Q16Sjm 1993
    [E]—dc20   92-34077

This North American library edition published in 1993 by Gareth
Stevens Publishing, 1555 North RiverCenter Drive, Suite 201, Milwaukee, Wisconsin 53212, USA, under an arrangement with Parents Magazine Press, New York.

Printed in the United States of America

1 2 3 4 5 6 7 8 9 98 97 96 95 94 93

SHERLOCK CHICK AND THE GIANT EGG MYSTERY

by Robert Quackenbush

PARENTS MAGAZINE PRESS · NEW YORK
Copyright ©1988 by Robert Quackenbush.

GARETH STEVENS PUBLISHING · MILWAUKEE

A Parents Magazine
Read Aloud Original

For Piet

Sherlock Chick,
the great detective,
was out walking one day
when he saw a big box.
"I wonder what this could be,"
he said.

Along came Sherlock Chick's
friends, Squeakins Mouse
and Charlie Chipmunk.
"What's in the box?"
they asked.

Just then, one side
of the box plopped open.
Out rolled a giant egg!

Sherlock Chick and his
friends were surprised.
"What kind of egg is that?"
asked Charlie Chipmunk.
"I don't know,"
said Sherlock Chick.
"I'll go get my mother.
She knows about eggs."
He ran to the chicken coop
to find Emma Hen.

"My goodness!" said Emma Hen.
"I've never seen such a big egg.
It needs warming so whatever
is inside can hatch.
A mother knows these things."
She climbed up on the
egg and sat down.

"This isn't going to work,"
said Emma Hen.
"The egg is much too big
for me to keep warm
all by myself."
"We'll help you!"
said Squeakins Mouse
and Charlie Chipmunk.
They climbed up on
the egg with her.

While the three of them
were busy on the egg,
Sherlock Chick went
to have another look
at the box.
He was hoping to
find some clues.
He wanted to solve the
mystery of the giant egg.

FROM
AUNT MATILDA
AFRICA

FOR FARMER
JONES
U.S.A.

Sherlock Chick walked
around the box.
On the back he found a label.
Now he knew that the egg
was for Farmer Jones.
And he knew it came from
Aunt Matilda in Africa.

Further along, Sherlock Chick
saw four stamps.
One showed a lion.
One showed a gorilla.
One showed an elephant.
And one stamp was torn.
All that could be seen were
two feet and the letters "ich."
"Hmmm," said Sherlock Chick.
"I wonder what an *ich* is."

Sherlock Chick went back
to the others.
"I found out that the egg
came from Africa," he said.
"And there were stamps on
the box showing a lion,
a gorilla, and an elephant."
Squeakins, Charlie, and
Emma Hen gasped.
"What if there's a lion
inside the egg?" said Squeakins.
"Or a gorilla?" said Emma Hen.
"Or an elephant?" said Charlie.

"Lions! Gorillas! Elephants!"
shouted Emma Hen.
"Run for your lives!"
yelled Squeakins.
They all jumped off
the egg and ran.

"Come back!" said
Sherlock Chick.
"Lions, gorillas, and elephants
don't hatch from eggs.
Besides, I also saw a
stamp with an animal
called an ich."

"My boy!" said Emma Hen.
"Of course you are right
about the other animals.
But what in the world
is an ich?"
"It makes me feel like
scratching," said Squeakins.
"That's an itch,"
said Sherlock Chick.
"If we all keep warming
the egg, perhaps we will
find out what is inside."
This time, Sherlock
sat on the egg, too.

They sat on the egg
for a long time.
Then Emma Hen said,
"I feel something moving."
The others felt it, too.

The egg was cracking open.
The four sitters
jumped off at once.
And in the nick
of time, too!
The shell broke apart
and out came...

...A *giant* baby bird!

"My goodness!" said Emma Hen.

"What a big ich!"

Sherlock Chick studied the bird.

Then he remembered a picture

he had seen in one of his books.

"This bird is not an ich!"

he said.

"Then what is it?"

asked the others.

"This bird is a baby ostrich,"
said Sherlock Chick.
"Only the last three letters
of his name were on the stamp.
The rest of his name
was torn off."

"What a smart detective
you are!"
said Emma Hen.
"And won't Farmer Jones be
surprised when he sees
the baby ostrich,"
said Squeakins.
"No more than us,"
said Sherlock Chick.
"After all...

...we hatched him!"

Notes to Grown-ups

Major Themes

Here is a quick guide to the significant themes and concepts at work in *Sherlock Chick and the Giant Egg Mystery:*

- Looking carefully: Sherlock Chick looked very slowly and closely at the big egg in the box to find the clues he needed to solve the mystery.
- Working together: sometimes, problems or little mysteries can best be solved by working together like Sherlock and his friends.

Step-by-step Ideas for Reading and Talking

Here are some ideas for further give-and-take between grown-ups and children. The following topics encourage creative discussion of *Sherlock Chick and the Giant Egg Mystery* and invite the kind of open-ended response that is consistent with many contemporary approaches to reading, including Whole Language:

- Like all detective stories, this book expects the reader to try to solve the mystery. As you read it, you can stop and ask your child what might be going to happen. What could possibly come from Africa? How big must a creature be to have such a huge egg? What might an "ich" be?
- Sherlock's friends are afraid the egg might contain a lion. This is a good time to talk about who lays eggs. All birds do, as do most fish (a few hatch them inside themselves), most snakes and other reptiles, all frogs, insects, and the unusual duck-billed platypus. But the creatures that we commonly think of as pets or farm animals have young in the form of puppies, kittens, cubs, calves, piglets, foals, and fawns.

Games for Learning

Games and activities can stimulate young readers and listeners alike to find out more about words, numbers, and ideas. Here are more ideas for turning learning into fun:

Feely Socks

Children use touch as a way of discovering what things really are. You will often see children reaching out both hands to examine something new, even though they are saying "let me *see* that." Children often don't feel they have really *seen* something until they have had an opportunity to touch it or play around with it for a while in their hands.

To sharpen tactile skills, a "feely sock" is a great way to create a mystery out of everyday objects and bring out the detective in your child. Simply take a large and fairly thick sock and, when your child is not looking, put an object inside, such as a spoon, a toy, a shoelace, a marker, or a spool of thread. Let your child reach in and touch the object without looking. Then see if your child can guess what is in the sock. Repeat with other objects.

Variation:

Let your child make some "feely socks" and try to fool you, siblings, or friends. There is an almost infinite variety of objects around the house that can be used to play this game.

About the Author/Artist

ROBERT QUACKENBUSH was thinking about how children are surprised and delighted by presents — the unexpected box, the mysterious contents — when he heard that many farmers are looking for new animals and crops to raise. "What might they grow?" wondered Mr. Quackenbush. So Sherlock Chick provided an answer.

Mr. Quackenbush is the author and illustrator of over 150 books for children.

E ✓   93-442
Quackenbush
   Sherlock Chick

93-442

Central Boulevard School
Central Boulevard
Bethpage, NY